MW00884884

To our beloved grandparents, Jack and Thelma, for all the wonderful times we spent together.

www.mascotbooks.com

Charlie Tractor and the Big Fish

©2018 Carrie Weyler and Katie Weyler. All Rights Reserved. No part of this publication may be reproduced, stored in a retrieval system or transmitted in any form by any means electronic, mechanical, or photocopying, recording or otherwise without the permission of the author.

For more information, please contact:
Mascot Books
620 Herndon Parkway, Suite 320
Herndon, VA 20170
info@mascotbooks.com

Library of Congress Control Number: 2018901150

CPSIA Code: PRT0318A
ISBN-13: 978-1-68401-436-1

Printed in the United States

CHARLIE™ TRACTOR
and THE BIG FISH

Carrie & Katie Weyler

illustrated by Rachel Schwarting

It was finally Saturday! Charlie was excited to visit Grandpa Jack and Grandma Thelma.

"Charlie, are you ready to go?" his mom asked.

"Yep!" answered Charlie eagerly. Charlie's grandparents lived on a farm just outside of town and it was Charlie's favorite place to visit in the whole world!

"Yippee! We're here!" Charlie hollered as Pickles barked in the background.

Charlie hopped out of the car with excitement, and Grandma Thelma greeted him with a big hug.

"And who is this?" Grandma asked with a smile, petting Charlie's four-legged friend.

"This is my new dog, Pickles!" Charlie replied happily.

"What do you want to do today?" Grandpa asked.

"Maybe ride the tractor around with you and go fishing in the pond!" Charlie answered with a grin.

"That sounds like a great plan!" Grandpa agreed.

"Oh no, I forgot my tackle box!" Charlie exclaimed.
"Do you have any fishing bait, Grandpa?"

"I sure do. I have all different kinds!" Grandpa replied.

"**Wow!**" Charlie yelled. "Can we ride your big green tractor?"

"You don't want to squeeze into my little blue one?" Grandpa asked with a laugh.

Charlie could barely tear his eyes away from the big green tractor, even just to look at the small blue one. "Just teasing you!" Grandpa said, grinning. "Of course we can ride the big green tractor."

Charlie, Pickles, and Grandpa loaded up their fishing gear and headed toward the pond.

"I'm going to catch the biggest fish you've ever seen, Grandpa!" Charlie shouted.

"We'll see about that!" Grandpa replied playfully.

As Charlie and Grandpa sat quietly by the water, waiting for the fish to bite, Pickles started getting restless.

He jumped onto Charlie and started to bark, licking his face and trying to play.

"Pickles!" Charlie whispered. "Be quiet! You're scaring the fish!"

"Grandpa," Charlie said, staring at the still water. "I don't think the fish like our worms. Do you have some other bait we can try?"

"Hmm…" Grandpa murmured, thinking.
"Let's try a minnow."

The fish didn't seem to like the minnows either,
so Charlie tried putting a grub on his hook.
Still, there were no fish biting.

"Grandpa, do you think fish like crickets?"
Charlie wondered.

"I don't know Charlie, but let's try it,"
Grandpa answered.

After what seemed like forever, there were still no fish biting.

"Well, the fish may not be hungry, but I sure am!" laughed Grandpa.

"Me too!" replied Charlie as his stomach rumbled.

Grandpa opened the picnic basket and handed Charlie a sandwich that Grandma Thelma had made for them. "A cheese sandwich?" Charlie asked excitedly. "That's my favorite kind!"

As Grandpa and Charlie ate their sandwiches, Pickles jumped up and down trying to sneak a bite. Charlie gave Pickles a small piece of his sandwich.

"Look Grandpa, Pickles likes cheese sandwiches as much as I do!"

"Do you think fish like cheese sandwiches?" Charlie continued. He wadded up a piece of his sandwich into a dough ball and put it on his hook.

"Well your Grandma Thelma makes the very best cheese sandwiches ever, so I bet they would!" Grandpa Jack proclaimed.

Suddenly, Charlie felt a strong tug on his fishing pole. Pickles barked excitedly as a huge fish jumped up out of the water at the end of Charlie's fishing pole.

"Reel it in, Charlie!" Grandpa exclaimed. "That's the biggest fish I've ever seen in this pond! Great job!"

"I can't wait to show Grandma!" Charlie hollered, holding the big fish he caught with pride.

It was such a great day fishing in Grandpa Jack's pond. Charlie couldn't wait for tomorrow's adventure!

THE END

About the Authors

Sisters Katie and Carrie Weyler, grew up in Ohio. Katie is the oldest of five children, while Carrie is the youngest. They had a fun and adventurous upbringing, which inspired the stories of Charlie Tractor™.

Now, with families of their own, they have set out to retell the stories they imagined and experienced as children. These stories, based on actual events, share the adventures of Charlie Tractor™ and his family.

They hope that these stories bring enjoyment and laughter to you and your family as much as they did to Katie and Carrie.

ABOUT THE CHARLIE TRACTOR™ BOOK SERIES

These short, fun, colorful books were created for busy parents, grandparents, teachers, and others with children two to ten years old. The adventures of Charlie Tractor™ are happy, simple, family-oriented stories designed to hold the child's attention, teach a fun fact or two, bring laughter and enjoyment, and be read in less than ten minutes.

Connect with us at:
www.charlietractor.com
charlietractorbooks@gmail.com
Follow us on Facebook and Instagram

Have a book idea?
Contact us at:

info@mascotbooks.com | www.mascotbooks.com